RABBIT ON THE RUN

by Ivan Cohen
illustrated by Dave Alvarez

PICTURE WINDOW BOOKS
a capstone imprint

Published by Picture Window Books,
an imprint of Capstone
1710 Roe Crest Drive
North Mankato, Minnesota 56003
capstonepub.com

Library of Congress Cataloging-in-Publication Data
Names: Cohen, Ivan, author. | Aesop. | Alvarez, Dave, illustrator.
Title: Rabbit on the run / by Ivan Cohen ; illustration by Dave Alvarez. Other titles: Looney Tunes.
Description: North Mankato, Minnesota : Picture Window Books, an imprint of Capstone, [2021] | Series: Looney Tunes wordless graphic novels | Audience: Ages 5-7. | Audience: Grades K-2. | Summary: "Bugs Bunny thinks he has the race in the bag when a slowpoke enters the triathlon. But who will win the classic showdown between the tortoise and the hare?"—Provided by publisher.
Identifiers: LCCN 2021002635 (print) | LCCN 2021002636 (ebook) | ISBN 9781663910066 (hardcover) | ISBN 9781663920324 (paperback) | ISBN 9781663910035 (ebook pdf)
Subjects: LCSH: Graphic novels. | CYAC: Graphic novels. | Stories without words. | Bugs Bunny (Fictitious character)—Fiction. | Racing—Fiction. | Turtles—Fiction.
Classification: LCC PZ7.7.C64 Rab 2021 (print) | LCC PZ7.7.C64 (ebook) | DDC 741.5/973—dc23
LC record available at https://lccn.loc.gov/2021002635
LC ebook record available at https://lccn.loc.gov/2021002636

Designed by Dina Her

Printed and bound in China. 5070

4
1

BUGS BUNNY AND TORTOISE

Bugs Bunny

Bugs is a tall gray-and-white rabbit who takes charge of any situation he finds himself in. Always curious about whatever is going on around him, he never says no to a challenge. While Bugs' enthusiasm often puts him in hot water, his quick wit and sense of humor are usually all he needs to get home safely.

Tortoise

Tortoise is a green-and-brown turtle who never gives up. His slow and steady ways often put him at the back of the pack. But while others get distracted, his determination always keeps him right on target.

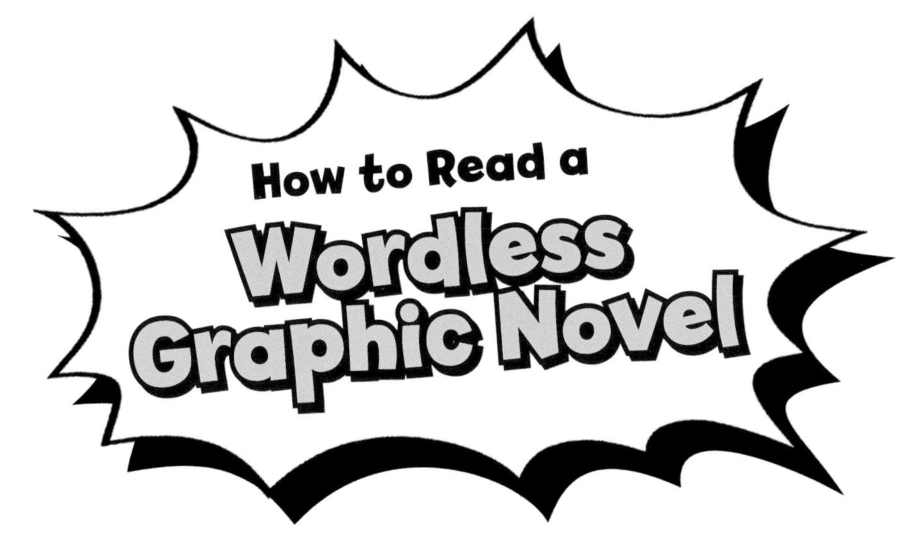

Wordless graphic novels are easy to read. Boxes called panels show you how to follow the story. Look at the panels from left to right and top to bottom. Read any sound effects as you go.

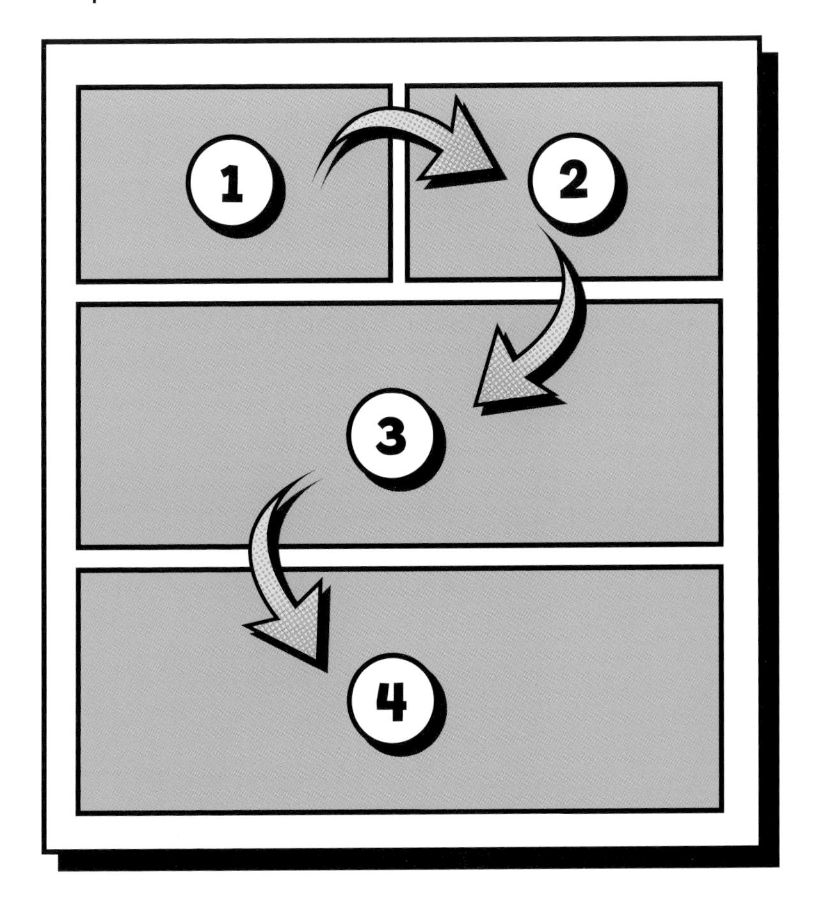

By putting the panels together, you'll understand the whole story!

Triathalon
Signup

WHAT'S UP DOC?

HUH?

DING!

HA HA HA HA!

TAP-TAP!

HAR HAR HAR!!

HA
HA HA
HA!
1
HEE
HEE HEE!

1
4
2
7

WHEE-EEE-EEET!
7

THUNK!

1
WHE-EEE-EET

WHOOOOSH!
2

SPLISH!
GLUB
SPLOOSH!

WHIRRRRRR!!!

ZOOOOM!

FINISH

HUMPH
GRRRR

WHEE-EEE-EEET!

WIZZ-WIZZ-WIZZZZ

B-BONK!

2
WAHHHH?

?

pedal
pedal
pedal

1
4

?!?!

YIII!

BOING!

TOODLE-OOO!

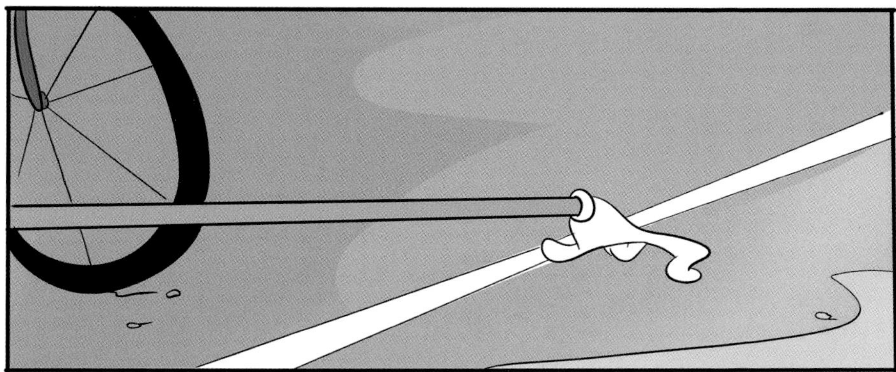

POP!

E LOONEY TIMES
RUN-OFF!
TORTOISE VS HARE
1
1
4

GULP
GULP
GULP!
4
1

WHEE-EEE-EEET!

SWOOOSH!

ACME
PRODUCTS
HONK-
HONK!!

?!?!

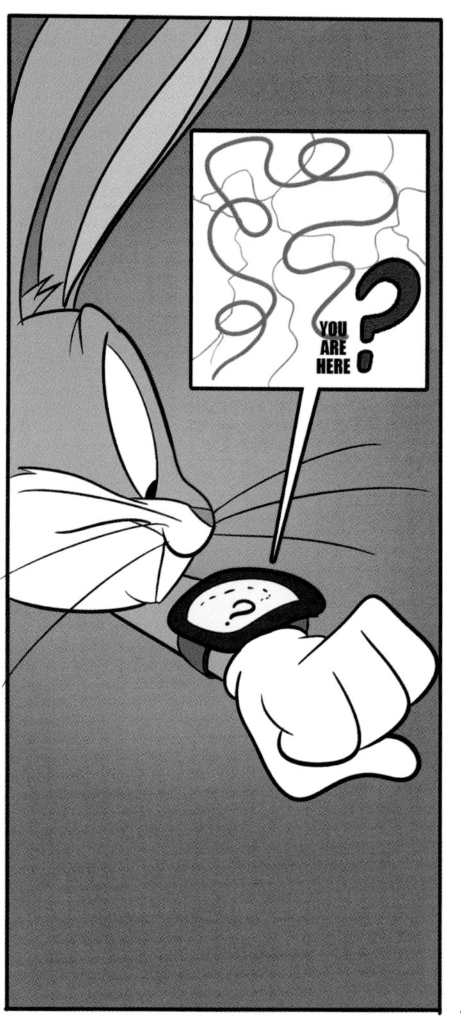
YOU ARE HERE
?

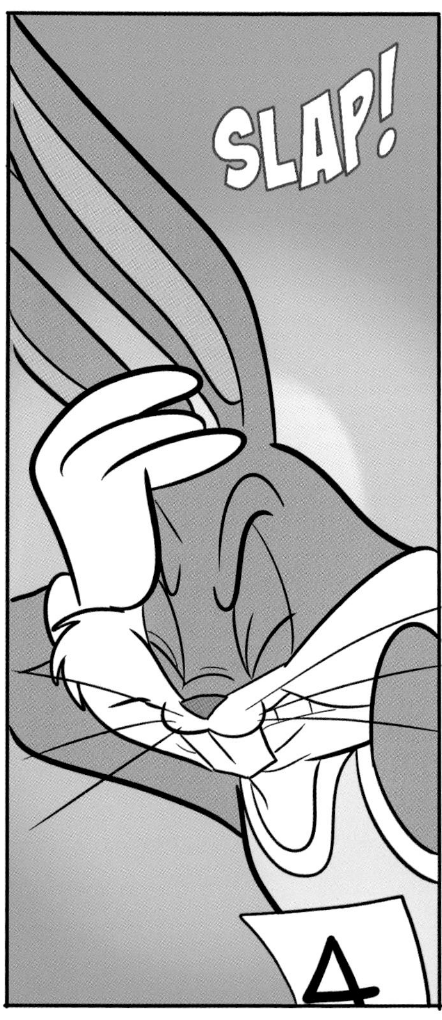
SLAP!

HONK-
HONK!!
ACME
PRODUCTS

Finish line
that-a-way

n Line
a-way

???

HAW HAW HAW!!!
START
1
HUH?
4

that-a-way
YAWWWWWN

ZZZZZZZZZZZ

BRRRR
ZZZZZZZZZZZ

ZZZZZZZZZZZZ
ZZZZZZZZZ

ZZZZ

GLUG!
GLUG! GLUG!

KA-POW!

WEE-OOO
WEE-OOO

WEE-OOO
WEE-OOO
FINSH LINE
4
1

GRAND CHAMPION
4

Panel Talk

1. Why is Bugs Bunny laughing at Tortoise in this panel? What do you think Elmer Fudd is thinking?

2. How do Bugs and Daffy Duck feel about Tortoise winning the race? What clues tell you that?

3. What is Bugs thinking about? How does he feel about his daydream?

4. Why are Daffy, Foghorn Leghorn, and the Tasmanian Devil pouring coffee in Bugs' mouth?

Through the Years

Looney Tunes has entertained fans both young and old for more than 90 years. It all started back in 1930 with animated short films that ran in movie theaters. By 1970, these shorts leaped from big movie screens to small TV screens. From that point forward, generations of young fans have grown up watching these classic cartoons in their own homes.

What makes Looney Tunes so successful? Its amazing cast of characters, of course! Stars include Bugs Bunny, Porky Pig, Daffy Duck, Tweety, Sylvester, Marvin the Martian, Road Runner, and Wile E. Coyote. And don't forget their outrageous costars! Elmer Fudd, Yosemite Sam, Foghorn Leghorn, Pepé Le Pew, and the Tasmanian Devil add hilarious hijinks to every story.

With such a zany cast, it's no wonder Looney Tunes' return to the big screen often bursts beyond straight animation. Modern films have featured Bugs Bunny and his friends mixing things up with live-action sports and movie stars in *Space Jam* and *Looney Tunes: Back in Action*. And in 2021, the film *Space Jam: A New Legacy* has them destined for even more out-of-this-world adventures!

About the Author

Ivan Cohen has written comics, children's books, and TV shows featuring some of the world's most popular characters, including Teen Titans Go!, Batman, Spider-Man, Wonder Woman, Superman, the Justice League, and the Avengers. Ivan looks forward to reading this book with his wife and son in their home in New York City.

About the Illustrator

Dave Alvarez is an artist and animator for several companies, including Warner Brothers Animation, Walt Disney Television, Netflix, DC Comics, IDW, and Nickelodeon. His work can be seen on productions like *Scooby Doo and Guess Who?*, *Looney Tunes*, *SpongeBob Squarepants*, *Tom and Jerry*, and others. In the comic book world, he's mostly known for his work on the Looney Tunes, Garfield, and Teenage Mutant Ninja Turtles series.